Mr. Bingley Plans a Ball

A TEATIME TALES
NOVELETTE

LEENIE BROWN

Leenie B Books
Halifax

ISBNs: 978-1-989410-73-8 (ebook); 978-1-990607-46-2 (print); 978-1-990607-47-9 (large print)

www.leeniebbooks.com

www.leeniebrown.com

Chapter 1

CHARLES BINGLEY STRAIGHTENED HIS sleeves and brushed a hand down the front of his coat as he removed as many of the signs of travel from his clothing as he could. He drew a deep breath and studied the flat façade of the stately home with its evenly spaced windows. Within these walls lay his happy future. Or so he hoped.

Movement at the sitting room window, as one of the pretty Bennet ladies peeked out and then ducked out of sight, caught his eye. From the quick glimpse he got of her – brown curls, green ribbons, no spectacles or sharp angles – he guessed it was Kitty.

He had been seen. There was no turning back now. He was here, at the border of the plain on which he would discover his destiny. Delight at being returned to Miss Bennet mingled with a flutter of nerves about being accepted by her as more than just any old caller.

Flutters or no, he must move forward into the fray, and so, he stepped up to the door. However, he did pause for a moment before ringing the bell to gather his confidence. No matter what his friend had said, Miss Bennet favoured him. He was not seeing things only as he wished them to be.

That friend, Fitzwilliam Darcy, would not be best pleased to read the missive that had surely reached Darcy House by now. There were very few times when Bingley had not taken Darcy's advice. Each of those times had been when Bingley had known to the core of his being that he was correct and his friend was wrong. This was one of those times. Darcy's opinion was clouded, but Bingley would see to the removal of those clouds.

Darcy was not the only one who would be displeased with Bingley's return to Hertfordshire. His younger sister, Caroline, would be appalled to hear of his whereabouts when she finally emerged from her bedchamber and was denied the use of the carriage because it was not in town.

He almost wished he could be at home to witness Caroline's displeasure or at Darcy House to see the look of horror which would surely wash over his friend's face when he read the contents of the letter Bingley had sent. However, he was – obviously – not at home. Instead, he was on a mission to see both himself and his dearest friend in all the world, happily situated with wives whom they adored.

He rang the bell as he chuckled to himself at how absolutely outraged Caroline would be that she had not prevented the loss of Darcy as she had intended by returning to town early. Maybe he would invite her to his ball, and maybe, he might even allow her to remain at Netherfield for the full twelve days of Christmas. That is, he might allow her if he were to begin feeling charitable towards her, though he doubted he would be feeling so any time soon. She could stay with Hurst and Louisa. It was best if she began her season as she should, which was by knowing that she needed to look for a husband who was not the master of Pemberley in Derbyshire.

His younger sister had demanded her way about many things over the years, and Bingley had capitulated to many of her demands. However, separating him from Miss Bennet and insisting that he forget her was a step too far for Bingley to abide – even from Caroline.

The door opened, and Bingley stepped inside Longbourn.

"Mr. Bingley to see Mr. Bennet." He placed his hat on the entryway table and handed his greatcoat to a footman.

"If you will follow me, sir."

Bingley followed Mr. Hill, Longbourn's butler, down the short hall which led to his master's study and waited in the corridor while permission was gained for him to enter.

"Mr. Bingley, please do come in and have a seat." Mr. Bennet stood behind his desk and motioned to the chairs in front of him. "I must confess my surprise at being called on by you. I had not thought we would see you again."

Bingley smiled as he arranged himself in what had to be the most uncomfortable chair in which he had ever sat. The back was too straight and the seat was far too firm. "I imagine my sisters' and friend's departure made it appear as if I would not return."

"That and the letter my daughter received."

Bingley's head tipped. "What letter?"

"From Miss Bingley. She intimated to Jane that you were to return to Netherfield no more this winter."

The brazenness of his sister's treachery deepened Bingley's resolve to stay separated from her. There would be no invitation to her or the Hursts. He would celebrate his Christmas with his new acquaintances in his new neighbourhood, and with Darcy and his sister, if the man would deign to attend him at Netherfield as requested.

"If Caroline had her way," he said to Mr. Bennet, "I would not have returned. I am afraid she favours town to the country."

Mr. Bennet's eyes searched him. "And does your friend also prefer London's society to that in Hertfordshire?"

Bingley laughed, despite his feeling of unease at Mr. Bennet's continued scrutiny. "My friend prefers a small group of friends and books to the frivolities of the ton or the charm of a country soiree." He paused. "I dare say that might be something the two of you have in common."

Mr. Bennet chuckled. "Indeed. I do prefer my solitude to a soiree, but I doubt very much that you came here to talk to me about my penchant for books over people. Would I be wrong to assume your visit is about one of my daughters – Jane, perhaps?"

The welcoming tone in which the question was asked dissolved the small bit of trepidation Bingley still held about the purposes of his call today. Feeling heartened, Bingley relaxed into his seat, rested his elbows on the arm of the chair, and steepled his fingers in front of his chest. "You would not be wrong, but you would also not be correct."

Mr. Bennet's head tipped, and a single eyebrow rose in intrigue. "A riddle in reply? I begin to see why your friend enjoys your company. You are not just an eager pup. It seems a shrewd mind lies behind your amiable façade."

Ah, yes. How many saw his happy manners and assumed that pleasantness and merriment were the only things of which he was capable? Fortunately, Darcy had been one of the few who had taken the care to look beyond Bingley's smile. Perhaps that was because Darcy, himself, was often assumed to be only serious and void of deep emotions because of his reserved nature.

"Most wonder at our friendship," Bingley admitted. "However, that is because most only see us in society, which, by the by, is the only place where my friend does not outshine me."

"You do seem an odd pair."

"What appears to be true is not always what is; or perhaps, it is true, and I prefer to surround myself with the unusual because life is more interesting that way. However, I suppose the real question is, could it be both?"

Mr. Bennet placed his spectacles on top of his book. "While I am curious to know the answer to that, I have a question of my own. Would you be seeking to add me to your collection of eccentrics by joining your family to mine?"

In spite of Bingley's certainty of being accepted, his hands suddenly felt sweaty, and he found it necessary to draw a deep breath before answering. "I would, sir, if that is acceptable to all parties."

"I cannot see how it would be unacceptable. You seem a decent sort of fellow, and I suspect you have the funds to provide for a family." Here, Mr. Bennet paused and waited for confirmation that his supposition was correct.

"I do."

"And while you have not said so, I assume you care for Jane?"

Bingley nodded. "Very much, sir."

"To the point of love?"

"Yes."

"Well, then, I must accept you, for if my wife were to hear that I refused your suit on my daughter's behalf when you have both a fortune and a deep admiration for her, not even this study would give me peace." Mr. Bennet laughed, and Bingley joined him.

"The final decision will, of course, be left to Jane," Mr. Bennet continued.

"Of course."

"Now, according to your earlier riddle, Jane is not your only reason for calling, is she?"

Bingley shook his head. "You would be correct. Permission to marry Miss Bennet is not the sole purpose of this interview, though her happiness and my own are the foundations for it."

Mr. Bennet chuckled. "Do you always speak in riddles, young man?"

While Bingley did not always speak in riddles, he had found that doing so often helped him keep Darcy's attention because it presented a problem to solve.

"What other business might you have with me, aside from permission to present your offer of marriage to Jane, which might secure your happiness?" Mr. Bennet's brow furrowed. "Is there another suitor whom I should dissuade in his suit?"

"As far as I know, Miss Bennet does not have any other suitors, but be that as it may, there is another gentleman who needs removal."

"Another gentleman?"

Bingley nodded.

"But he is not a suitor?" Mr. Bennet was beginning to look slightly frustrated, which meant it was time for Bingley to present his second purpose plainly.

"I am speaking of Mr. Wickham."

Mr. Bennet's already furrowed brow knit further. "What of Mr. Wickham? He seems a pleasant sort of fellow, though he is not so well-liked by your friend."

"For good reason, sir. This is another time when what appears to be and what is are not the same. As you say, Mr. Wickham appears to be a pleasant and proper gentleman when, in fact, he is given to gambling and debauchery. If he is living as he usually does, I would suspect that several in Meryton hold his vowels and more than one maid is a maiden no longer." He let his words settle into the silence of the room.

Horror washed over Mr. Bennet's features. "Truly?" he finally asked.

"I assure you, sir, that I speak with authority and no exaggeration. His tales of my friend are cunningly crafted with enough truth to make his defamatory comments believable."

"A practiced deceiver?"

Bingley nodded and leaned forward in his chair. "I do not know what Wickham has told you about his relationship with Darcy, but please, allow me to share the high points of their history."

Mr. Bennet motioned with his hand for Bingley to continue.

"Wickham grew up at Pemberley. His father was the estate's steward. When Mr. Darcy died, he left Wickham an inheritance. It was a valuable living which would be his upon his taking orders and the living falling open. Wickham, however, did not think the church would suit him and refused the living, opting instead to take a monetary settlement in its place. It was not a small settlement, but it was quickly squandered. Wickham then returned to take up the living, which had recently fallen open. Darcy refused him."

"I should think he would refuse!" Mr. Bennet cried. "Is Mr. Wickham such a scoundrel then?"

"Much worse, I fear, and this part you must never share. As you know, Darcy has a sister."

Mr. Bennet closed his eyes and shook his head against the pain that etched his features.

"Darcy's sister is the same age as Miss Lydia."

Again, Mr. Bennet shook his head with his eyes still closed.

"Wickham attempted to seduce her for her dowry."

Mr. Bennet expelled a great breath. "Do you believe my daughters are in danger from this man?" he asked after opening his eyes.

"I do."

"But they have very little."

"He does not seek their money."

Mr. Bennet's eyes grew wide.

Bingley nodded. "It is not just your daughters' virtues which are at stake here. The happiness of my friend and Miss Elizabeth is also in danger."

"Mr. Darcy and Elizabeth?"

Bingley allowed Mr. Bennet to ponder the match.

"They would do well together," Mr. Bennet admitted after some contemplation. "However, your friend finds my daughter merely tolerable, and she is so set against..." His voice trailed off, and a smile suffused his face. "She is enamoured with him! How did I not see it before?"

"I cannot speak to Miss Elizabeth's feelings about my friend, but I can assure you that he finds her a great deal more than tolerable." He gave Mr. Bennet a wry smile.

"His comments at the assembly were part of a game we play. Or, I should say, a game I play, and Darcy endures. I encourage him to interact with people, and he attempts to put me off by telling me the exact opposite of what he is truly thinking."

Mr. Bennet raised an eyebrow and gave a little chuckle.

"Though he is reluctant to admit it, Darcy has never been so enamoured. In fact, he would like to introduce his sister to Miss Elizabeth. However, Miss Darcy will not be allowed to travel to Netherfield while Wickham is in Hertfordshire."

It was Darcy's fear that Wickham might do some harm to the Bennets because of his or Bingley's connection to them which had been his impetus for his leaving Netherfield and discouraging the match between Bingley and Miss Bennet. That was not information which had been easily uncovered. It had taken some yelling and threatening before Darcy gave it up.

Mr. Bennet nodded slowly as he absorbed all that had been presented to him. "And you have told me all you have about Wickham so that I can make known his real character in an attempt to force him from the area."

"That is the plan. If all goes well, I shall host a Yuletide ball to celebrate my betrothal to Miss Bennet. Darcy will, of course, attend, and he and his sister will join me for Christmas." Or so Bingley hoped. "And then, well, then, I suppose, we shall see what can be done about improving Miss Elizabeth's opinion of my friend."

"Well, then." Mr. Bennet stood and straightened his jacket. "I feel a need to visit my friend Sir William and share some gossip concerning a particular officer." He lifted a hand to forestall Bingley's comments. "I shall not reveal my source, nor will I mention the attempted seduction."

"I had not thought you would, sir. I was only going to agree that indeed, a little gossip might be our solution."

Mr. Bennet chuckled. "Do not let the parson hear you say so."

"I would not think to tell him."

"I suppose you had best be about your business with my daughter if we wish to announce a betrothal," Mr. Bennet said as he opened the door to his study, motioning for Bingley to exit ahead of him, which Bingley did.

"Two sons – two wealthy sons," Mr. Bennet muttered softly as he followed behind Bingley. "Fanny shall surely go distracted!"

Chapter 2

"Mrs. Bennet." Mr. Bennet stood in the doorway to the sitting room with Bingley behind him. "One of your daughters has a caller, if she will see him."

"If she will see him?" Mrs. Bennet cried. "I dare say she will see him."

"Elizabeth," Mr. Bennet said.

"Elizabeth?" Mrs. Bennet turned her eyes from Bingley to Mr. Bennet. "Elizabeth?" she repeated.

For a moment, Bingley thought that perhaps the woman would faint away from the shock of hearing Miss Elizabeth's name.

"Did I say Elizabeth?" Mr. Bennet queried. "Forgive me. I meant Jane."

"Oh, my nerves! You do not know what you do to me." Mrs. Bennet sank back in her chair and, opening a fan which she had retrieved from the table next to her, she fanned herself.

Mr. Bennet chuckled.

Bingley was certain that the man knew exactly what he did to his wife, and though her words had sounded sharp, the way she glanced at her husband from behind her fan did not speak of a lady who was utterly put out at all.

"Jane, my dear," Mr. Bennet continued.

Bingley looked in her direction. She was sitting with Miss Elizabeth, and her cheeks were a lovely shade of pink.

"Get your things. I have given Mr. Bingley permission to speak to you in private."

"In private!" Mrs. Bennet gasped, and her fan fluttered faster.

"I think it is just the sort of day on which a walk would be lovely, do you not think so, Mr. Bingley?"

"Yes, sir. That is a fine idea."

"I would stay to the back of the garden if I were you since it is harder to see from the windows in this room. However, there are other windows, so behave accordingly," Mr. Bennet whispered to Bingley while Miss Bennet gave Miss Elizabeth's hand a squeeze, and then, after some quiet communication between the two, Miss Bennet rose and crossed the room.

Both Bingley and Mr. Bennet stepped to the side to allow her to exit.

"Miss Bennet," Bingley said with a nod of his head in greeting.

"Mr. Bingley." She dipped the shallowest of curtseys before beginning to ascend the stairs. Halfway up she looked back and smiled when she saw that Bingley was still watching her.

"I am off to see Sir William. There will be no going to town or entertaining officers while I am out."

"No officers!" Miss Lydia cried. "But what if they come to our door? Are we to turn them away?"

"I would not be opposed to that," Mr. Bennet replied.

"Mr. Bennet," Mrs. Bennet said, "it would be dreadfully unfriendly of us to do so."

Mr. Bennet took his hat from Mr. Hill. "Very well, since we do not wish to have it said we are uncordial, you may entertain them in here. There will, however, be no private walks, save for Jane's walk with Mr. Bingley."

"Papa!" Miss Lydia cried in displeasure once again.

"I will hear nothing more on the subject." He looked to his wife. "I will be home well before dinner." Then, he gave her a nod of his head and took his leave.

"Mr. Bingley," Mrs. Bennet said from her place in the sitting room, "after you have walked in the garden, you will join us for a cup of tea, will you not?"

He could hear Miss Bennet's light steps as she descended the stairs, and he wished to turn to look at her. It took some effort to keep attending Mrs. Bennet. "I hope to."

Mrs. Bennet's smile grew, "Do not let me keep you."

"I am ready," Miss Bennet said softly.

Bingley slipped into his greatcoat, placed his hat on his head, and extended his arm to her.

"I am not being an imposition, am I?" he asked softly when she placed her hand on his arm.

"No."

"I am glad." His heart picked up its pace. He had expected her to be more openly welcoming, but her expression seemed guarded.

"I had not expected to see you," she said once they were out of the house.

Ah, that must be the source of her caution. "I promised I would return. However, your father informed me, much to my surprise, that my sister sent you a letter which indicated I would not be returning."

"Indeed, she did."

Again, it was not the response he was expecting. Miss Bennet was by no means exuberant, but he had hoped for at least a genuine smile rather than the polite one she wore. Perhaps she was not happy he had returned. Perhaps she did not admire him so much as he thought she did. Perhaps Darcy had been right about her indifference.

No, he could not believe that. It must be something else which troubled her.

"I admit I was angry with Caroline for returning to town as she did, but I am far more displeased to know she lied to you." He glanced at her. Still, she wore what appeared to be a practiced smile.

"Were you able to accomplish all the business that needed to be done while you were in town?"

"I was. I almost thought I might be held up an additional day by my solicitor, but arrangements were made so that I could return on the day I said I would."

"I am happy to hear it."

There was a small flash of pleasure in her expression before it fled.

"I hope you found Miss Darcy in good health," she said.

Bingley's brow furrowed. Miss Darcy? Why would she think he would see Miss Darcy? "I did not see her, but her brother did not mention anything was amiss when I saw him two days ago."

"You did not call on her?"

"No."

"Why not?"

What did she mean why not? "Why would I call on her?" Did she call on the brothers of all her friends? He highly doubted it.

"Is that not what a gentleman does when he hopes to court a lady?"

Bingley halted mid-stride. "I beg your pardon?"

Miss Bennet removed her hand from his arm and folded her gloved hands in front of her. "I asked if it was not customary for a gentleman to call on a lady he hopes to court." Her lashes fluttered over a hard stare. Even her polite smile was gone now.

"You think I wish to court Miss Darcy?"

"I do."

"What –? How –?" Bingley stammered. "Why do you think that? Did I not make my intentions toward you abundantly known?"

Her lips trembled for a moment, and her eyes glistened. "I had thought you did, but then, your sister said –"

"My sister?" Bingley interrupted far more loudly than he should have. "Did my sister tell you I was hoping to court Miss Darcy?"

Miss Bennet pressed her lips together, and her shoulders lifted and lowered in a deliberate breath. "She said you wished for more than a courtship."

Bingley's eyebrows flew up towards the brim of his hat while his eyes grew so wide that he thought they might drop out of his head.

"In the letter..." Miss Bennet looked down at her clasped hands.

"Of all the dreadful things Caroline has done!" He removed his hat and slapped it against his leg instead of uttering the curse that came to mind. He turned away from Miss Bennet and shook his head. "Do you think me so ungentlemanly as to practically declare myself to you when I am hoping to secure another?" He turned back to her.

She shook her head. "But Miss Bingley..." She pressed her lips together, and he could see her struggle to retain her composure play out on her face for a silent moment before she whispered, "I thought I had lost you." And then, all her efforts were for naught as tears began to trace trails down her beautiful face.

The sight tore at his heart, and, instinctively, he reached for her hand.

"I shall never love anyone but you." He brushed at her tears with his right hand while his left still held her hand. "You will have to send me away to be rid of me."

Her lips tipped into a small smile. A truly happy one.

"The business with my solicitor which nearly kept me away a day longer than planned was marriage papers."

Her smile grew, and he fished his handkerchief out of his pocket for her.

"I wanted to have them ready should I be so fortunate as to be successful in gaining the honour of your acceptance of my offer." He glanced at the house. They had only just entered the garden and were nowhere near the far corner her father had mentioned. As expected, several heads ducked out of sight. What did it matter if he had an audience? She would accept him, would she not?

He blew out a breath and then, went down on one knee.

"Miss Bennet, would you please make me the happiest man in the world by marrying me?" That was not precisely how he had planned to ask her, but in all the scenarios he had gone over his mind, he had never included his youngest sister being so cruel. "I will disown Caroline if need be," he added. Disowning Caroline was a tempting idea.

Miss Bennet laughed. "So long as she does not have to live with us, I think you can keep your sister."

So long as she does not live with us. Joy welled in Bingley's heart. "Does that mean you will marry me? I will send Caroline to Scotland if Hurst will not take her."

Her head bobbed up and down as fresh tears dampened her face. "Yes, yes, I will most happily marry you."

He rose and lifted her fingers to his lips. It was not how he had hoped to seal their understanding, but he did have an audience.

"Do you wish to return to the house?" he asked.

"No, I would rather walk with you." She interlaced her arm with his. "Unless, of course, you are cold and wish to return to the house."

"I am perfectly well, thank you."

They began walking away from the house and toward the back corner of the garden. Perhaps he might be able to steal a kiss after all.

"I would like to plan a ball to celebrate our betrothal."

"You do?"

"I do, but if I am being honest, and I promise I will never be anything but honest with you, our betrothal is only one of the reasons for my desire for a ball."

Her face turned towards him. "What other reasons do you have?"

"It is a matter of some delicacy and must be kept in confidence."

"From everyone?"

"Not your father, but yes, everyone else."

"I am intrigued, Mr. Bingley."

"Would you call me Charles?"

"Gladly, and you may call me Jane if you wish."

"I would love to call you Jane."

She moved closer towards him as they walked.

"I will not reveal your secret to anyone."

"Not even Miss Elizabeth?" Bingley knew that the two sisters were close. In fact, he was counting on that closeness to help him alter Miss Elizabeth's opinion of Darcy. "Most especially, not Miss Elizabeth."

"I will do my best."

It would have to do. He knew that she would not purposefully reveal his secret reason for planning a ball. Nearly from the moment he had met her, he had trusted her more than he had ever trusted anyone before in his life. She was open and unaffected. Added to that, she had a kind and tender heart. That was why he had been so certain that Darcy was wrong. Jane was not the sort of lady to lead a gentleman down a merry path just for the entertainment of it.

"My friend is enamoured with your sister," he whispered.

She gasped. "I knew it! I just knew it. Not that Elizabeth would believe me."

"Is she completely set against him?"

Jane's expression fell. It was all the answer he needed, but he waited to hear what she had to say.

"He did insult her."

"That was my fault, which I will explain to you, but is that the only reason?"

She shook her head. "She has heard stories about him that paint him in a very poor light."

"From Mr. Wickham?" He knew the answer before he asked the question, but he did not want to assume anything.

"Yes. I told her she should not listen to him, but she would not hear it."

Bingley blew out a breath. "She should not listen to him. Indeed, she should not speak to him at all – nor should your other sisters. He is a dangerous man."

Jane's hand flew to her heart. "How so?"

For the next twenty minutes, he and Jane strolled in the garden as he told her, in even greater detail than he had shared with Mr. Bennet, all he knew about Wickham.

"How am I not supposed to tell my sisters about this?" she asked when he had finished speaking.

"Your father and I will rid the area of him."

"What if he does not go? What if he discovers what you are about and tries to stop you?"

For all her serenity, there seemed to be a dash of her mother's nerves in Jane, and since they were in the far corner of the garden, he pulled her into his embrace. "Wickham will leave. Darcy will bring his sister to meet your sister, and all will be well, my love. All will be well." It had to be, for his own happiness would be forever tainted by the unhappiness of a friend if it were not.

Chapter 3

IN EARLY DECEMBER, SHADOWS, as day slid into night, enveloped the landscape and crept into the houses earlier and earlier with each passing day. It would be a dreary time of year if it were not for the prospect of Christmas. This year, the dreariness of the season promised to be dispelled in a much brighter fashion than most years.

As Bingley sat down at his desk in his study, a sense of satisfaction and a welling-up of pride in his position as the master of Netherfield settled upon him. He might only be the temporary master of Netherfield because he had not yet decided upon settling in the area permanently – for that was a decision he would not make without considering Jane's thoughts on the matter – however, he would be a proper master of his home while he was in residence.

"I have delightful news to share, Mrs. Nichols," he began. "We are having a ball."

His housekeeper's expression did not shift, save for the way she blinked. That flutter of lashes was the only thing which gave away her surprise at the news.

"I know it has not been long since the last ball, but I must celebrate my success in securing the prettiest lady in Hertfordshire as my future bride."

This time, his housekeeper smiled broadly in response to his announcement. "You are betrothed? To Miss Bennet?"

Bingley gave a nod of his head. "I am. Only just, but I am."

"That is excellent news, sir. My happiest wishes to both you and Miss Bennet."

"Thank you. I shall pass along your kind felicitations when I call on Miss Bennet tomorrow."

"When will the ball take place?" Mrs. Nichols' notebook was open, and her pencil was poised to record whatever notes needed to be made.

"Two days before Christmas."

"December 23," Mrs. Nichols said as she wrote down the date. "Three weeks is a good amount of time to prepare all that is needed. Will there be festivities to consider for the days after the ball and until Twelfth Night?"

"Yes, yes, I intend to celebrate the season completely."

Mrs. Nichols looked at him with an expression that he might be so bold as to call pride. "That is so good to hear, sir. It has been so long since we had a proper Christmas celebration. Will you have guests?"

That was an excellent question. "I have invited Mr. and Miss Darcy to stay with us. If they accept my invitation, I expect Miss Darcy to be accompanied by her companion, Mrs. Annesley."

This information was scratched down in the notebook.

"And your relations?"

"Will be remaining in town."

His housekeeper lifted her eyes from the page on which she was writing.

"I am quite put out with them," he said in answer to the question he was certain she wished to ask but would not for fear of being improper. "And there is the season for which to prepare. Therefore, it is best if they remain in town."

"I see. Then, it will be just you who will be making the plans for this ball?"

He shook his head. "I am certain Mrs. Bennet will wish to have some input as this is a soiree for her daughter." Or daughters if things went well. "We will need the ballroom cleaned and readied, of course, as well as the rest of the house, but I shall leave it to you to prepare a menu of what shall be served to our guests for you know best what is in the storehouses and what can be acquired. When it is ready, I would like to have a copy to take to Mrs. Bennet so that she and I can review it."

"I shall draw something up right away. Would the day after next be soon enough?"

That was about a day quicker than he had hoped. "That would be excellent."

"Shall I prepare the guest rooms immediately, or shall I wait until you have heard if Mr. Darcy and his sister will be joining you?"

"I think it would be wise to begin with the refreshing of those rooms." It was best to act as if his plan was a success. It would not do to enter into a scheme with doubts on display. One did not prepare for failure unless one wished to fail, and Bingley had no desire to fail.

"Very good, sir. Was there anything else?"

"Not at present. I will be dining at Longbourn tomorrow night."

"And would you like your dinner brought to you tonight, or do you prefer to eat in the dining room?"

"Bring it here."

He did not like dining by himself. Indeed, he did not know what he was going to do with himself for the whole evening. He had not considered being alone at Netherfield when he had decided to return without Darcy or his sister. He likely should have, but he had not. There was nothing to do now but to endure it.

He waited until Mrs. Nichols left before removing his jacket and unbuttoning his waistcoat. If he was to be alone, he might as well be comfortable.

He poked at the fire in the hearth before surveying the small room from which he would run all the affairs of his home. The adequately large, but not overly grand, mahogany desk seemed well-situated. He would leave that as is. However...

He took hold of one of the green upholstered chairs near the hearth and turned it. Why everyone wished to look into a crackling fire when they could be looking at the person to whom they were speaking, he would never know. He much preferred seeing the expression on his companion's face when having a discussion, for he could tell far more easily how the conversation was going if he could see their eyes widen or their mouth turn down into a scowl or up into a smile.

Having turned one chair, he proceeded to do the same with the other. That left the small octagonal table which had stood between the chairs. He would need another so that each person had a place to rest a glass of port or deposit a book. If he remembered correctly, there was a table very similar to, if not exactly the same as, this one in the library.

"Allow me to carry that for you," a footman offered when he saw Bingley carrying the second of the pair of matching octagonal tables down the corridor five minutes later.

"Thank you, Stewart, but I think I can manage the table. However, if you would make sure the door to my study is opened."

"Of course."

"There." Bingley stood the table next to the right side of the chair that was sitting alone in the grouping.

"May I assist you with anything else, sir?"

"I think I have everything I need."

Bingley chuckled to himself. He was certain he would hear about his rearranging the furniture from either Mr. Morris or Mrs. Nichols later. However, this was his house, and he had no sister here to tell him where things must remain.

He surveyed the room again. His cheeks puffed out and then flattened as he expelled the breath he had drawn. Maybe he should consider moving the desk, for there were still many hours between now and tomorrow morning. Or... he turned and looked at the door. No, Mrs. Nichols would likely not be fond of him pushing furniture around in every room just so he had something to do.

He dropped into one of the chairs near the hearth.

"What shall we do tonight?" he asked the chair across from him. "Mrs. Nichols knows about the ball..." He drummed his fingers on the arms of the chairs. "We could read." His nose wrinkled at the thought. "No, I do not wish to read either," he said, as if agreeing with his non-existent companion. He was far too restless to read tonight. "Billiards could be entertaining."

He pushed up from his chair. "Meryton could use a gentlemen's club."

He supposed there was a public house that would afford him some diversion – or, at least, noise. However, it would also likely be filled with militia, and if there were any games being played, Wickham would, without a doubt, be present. He had no wish to listen to that man.

As Bingley's lonely footsteps resounded down the corridor, he became resolved of one thing. A gentleman with a fortune and an estate needed a wife and neighbours to help fill the vast rooms and long corridors with something other than deafening quiet that was only broken by the scurrying of servants.

He shook his head. He was surrounded by people, waiting to fulfill his every request, and yet, he had no one to keep him company. He stopped just inside the billiards room. He was the master; he could remedy his present predicament. He poked his head out the door. "Stewart," he called.

"Yes, sir."

"Do you play billiards?"

"No, sir."

"Good. Then, I will teach you."

"Teach me, sir?"

Bingley nodded. "I am bored, and I would like for you to help relieve some of my boredom. Come now." He nodded to the interior of the billiard room.

However, before Stewart could enter the room, the sound of the door opening and the butler greeting someone reached Bingley.

"Our game may have to wait," he said to the footman, whose whole being seemed to sigh with relief as Bingley hurried down the hall, with Stewart following behind him, to see who might have arrived.

"I will only be staying the night. My business with Mr. Bingley is brief."

He knew that voice! He was in luck! Darcy would make the evening far less boring.

"Very good, Mr. Darcy," Mr. Morris replied. "I will see that your room is made ready."

"Darcy!" Bingley greeted his friend with delight. "I did not expect you until tomorrow."

Darcy stood with one arm in and one arm out of his greatcoat. "You were expecting me?"

"After that letter I left you, yes, I was." Bingley leaned against the newel post at the bottom of the staircase. "That is why you are here, is it not?"

"Yes, it is." Darcy handed his coat to Stewart, who had also been given Darcy's hat by the butler.

"Stewart," Bingley said.

The man looked at him apprehensively. "Yes, sir?"

"Make sure there is enough dinner brought to my study for both Mr. Darcy and me."

A smile tipped the man's lips. "Of course."

"Come, Darcy. You remember where the study is, do you not?"

"I have not been gone that long."

"No, but you have been gone, which makes me question your sense."

"Do not begin with me again. We canvassed this thoroughly the last time we were in company, although perhaps it was not canvassed so thoroughly as it should have been since I received this with my breakfast." He slapped the letter he held against Bingley's chest as he entered Bingley's study.

Bingley grabbed the letter. "I told you that I was returning to Netherfield and expected you to fulfill your promise to me before I left Darcy House that night."

"But you did not tell me that you were leaving today."

"I said I was returning just as soon as my business was concluded. I received what I needed last evening, and so here I am. My business is done, and I am returned to Netherfield just as I said I would. I am a man of my word, after all." He folded his arms across his chest and leaned against his desk. "However, thanks to my sister, Miss Bennet believed I was quite the opposite."

"What do you mean?" Darcy asked as he seated himself in a chair by the hearth. "These chairs would do better if they were facing the fire. The wings would keep the warmth in much better."

"And I would not be able to see your face. They are staying as they are, for this is my study."

Darcy's brow furrowed. "Are you still angry with me?"

Bingley sighed deeply and moved from his desk to the chair across from Darcy. "No. I am furious with my sister and will only be angry with you again if you knew anything about what she did."

"What did she do?" Darcy's eyes held that same wary expression Stewart had given Bingley.

"When she departed for town, Caroline left a letter for Miss Bennet."

"Yes, I know she did that."

"Do you know what was in it?" He was certain Darcy did not know, for Darcy had never once promoted a match between Bingley and Georgiana.

"I am sure I do not."

"She intimated that I would not be returning to Netherfield."

Darcy grimaced. "That was her desire."

"And yours, too." He gave Darcy a pointed look.

"Yes, it was mine as well."

"She also hinted that we were hopeful that a match between me and your sister was in the future."

Darcy's features became stony, and Bingley watched his friend's chest for the rise and fall of breathing. There was none until Darcy quickly inhaled through his nose.

"You and Georgiana?" he asked.

Bingley nodded. "You can imagine that my welcome from Miss Bennet was not what I had expected."

"You and Georgiana?" Darcy repeated.

Again, Bingley nodded.

"Where did she get that idea?"

"Surely you are not unaware of her desire to join our families."

"Through marrying me, not through your marrying my sister."

"Think for a moment, Darcy. What better way is there to ensure that Miss Bennet will give me up than to make her think I had toyed with her heart while all but betrothed to another?"

"But you would never do that."

"I know that. You know that. My sister knows that, but Miss Bennet did not. She knew I had left Netherfield, and that my friend and sisters had followed after me. She had nothing to go on but that wretched letter." Bingley shook his head. "She was in tears, Darcy. In. Tears."

Darcy closed his eyes. "I am sorry. Had I known…"

"I know. You would not have allowed such perfidy to happen. However, all is not lost. I explained myself, and I am to be married."

Darcy's eyes popped open. "Married? You settled it so soon?"

"There was no reason to wait in securing my happiness."

"But Wickham –"

"He will not be an issue."

"He is always an issue where I am concerned, and since you are my closest friend, that concern extends to you."

"He will not be a problem."

Darcy shook his head. "You cannot know that."

"I think I can."

"How?"

"I may have mentioned to Mr. Bennet that Wickham has a penchant for creating bills he never pays and seducing ladies. He is going to spread a few tales to those who might refuse to extend credit to Wickham, and to those who might wish to keep their daughters untainted."

Darcy's expression loudly proclaimed that he thought Bingley mad. "Gossip? You think you can run Wickham off with some gossip?"

Bingley nodded. "I do."

Again, Darcy's head was swinging from side to side in disagreement.

"He will run out of funds and go in search of some," Bingley explained. "Hopefully, he will not return when he does."

"I cannot believe it will work."

Bingley shrugged. "Only time will tell, my friend. Only time will tell."

"You will have to write to me with the details, for I am not staying longer than one night. I have only come in person to see that you are set up to conduct whatever needs doing between now and the new year. I will return in January for a visit, but I am not returning to Netherfield. Our discussions can be conducted by the post."

"You must come to my ball."

"What ball?"

"The one I am hosting two days before Christmas to celebrate my betrothal."

Darcy shook his head. "I am sorry, but I cannot. I will not leave Georgiana alone at Christmas time."

"You may bring her and Mrs. Annesley with you. I told you that in that letter."

"I know you did, but I do not think it is a good idea."

"Wickham will be gone."

"You cannot know that."

Bingley huffed in exasperation. "And you cannot know that I cannot know." Why could his friend not, just this once, have some faith in things not turning into a disaster?

"You are not making sense."

That was likely true but... "Neither are you."

"I did not come here to argue with you, Bingley. I came to go over books and answer questions."

"That will take longer than one night." Bingley knew that he was being very much like a petulant child, but frankly, he did not care. He needed Darcy to return to Netherfield. How was Miss Elizabeth supposed to change her opinion of the man if he was not here to show her that he was not what she thought he was? His left eyebrow arched, and a smile curled his lips.

"You know," he began, "Miss Bennet mentioned that Miss Elizabeth has been speaking to Wickham –" ah, there, he had Darcy's attention now, "– about you."

"About me?"

Bingley nodded. "And your sister."

"My sister?" The words rumbled from his friend. "What has the scoundrel said about my sister?"

"I did not ask. However, if you stay until after my call at Longbourn tomorrow, I will ask Miss Bennet." It was not much, but it might buy him one more day in which to work upon Darcy.

Darcy pondered the thought silently. "I will leave the day after tomorrow," he finally said as a tray of food was brought in.

Chapter 4

"MR. DARCY, IT IS a pleasure to see you, sir. I had not thought you were returning." Mr. Bennet handed the reins he held to a groom. The patriarch of the Bennet family had arrived at the front of Longbourn's manor house just moments after Bingley and Darcy had.

"Some extra attention for this lad today," he instructed the groom. "He has had a good run." Then, he turned back to Darcy.

"I am only here for a day or so to make certain Bingley is set with all that needs to be done until the new year."

Mr. Bennet's eyebrows rose in surprise, and he gave Darcy an appraising look. "You are not staying? I had thought you to be a closer friend to Mr. Bingley than that."

Bingley wanted to hug his future father-in-law, for there was a small smile tugging at the edges of the gentleman's mouth, and Bingley suspected that Mr. Bennet was attempting to aid in the cause to keep Darcy in Hertfordshire. Choosing to question Darcy's loyalty to a friend was guaranteed to provoke the man.

"I apologize," Darcy said brusquely, "but I do not understand your criticism of my plans."

"I am sure I did not mean to offend, sir. I am, however, certain if you think about it, you will see from whence my astonishment comes."

And posing the reply as something to be reasoned out was an excellent way to keep Darcy engaged in the conversation rather than allowing him to pass it by as unfounded foolishness spouted by those who were ignorant of who he was. Darcy did tend to think highly of himself at times. This unwavering response, which Mr. Bennet had given, was precisely the thing that was needed. Bingley had thought Mr. Bennet to be an intelligent fellow with a quick wit, and it appeared he was absolutely correct on that account. One or two mentions of how Darcy was similar to him had been enough for Mr. Bennet to know how to confound and draw Darcy along.

"I have had it from your mouth, Mr. Darcy, that Mr. Bingley is your dearest friend." Mr. Bennet continued as he took off his gloves and hat. "Come in. Come in." He nodded toward Longbourn and started walking toward the door, leaving little option but for Bingley and Darcy to follow him. "I would think that one dear friend would not refuse to share in the joy of the other." He stopped just before the door. "Mr. Bingley did tell you that he and Jane are to be married and that he is holding a ball to celebrate their betrothal, did he not?"

"He did, but –"

"I told Elizabeth that Wickham fellow was wrong about you, but perhaps it is I who was wrong," he said before Darcy could finish his reasons for not remaining at Netherfield.

Darcy's mouth snapped shut, and his chin lifted. "Whatever Wickham has said about me is most assuredly lies."

Mr. Bennet gave Darcy a skeptical look. "Mr. Wickham said you cared little for others, to put it gently. I had not seen it until now." And with that Mr. Bennet entered the house.

The accuracy of the resounding shot the man had fired with such a statement could be seen in the way Darcy pulled his shoulders up and back. Questioning his loyalty to his friends was high on Darcy's list of tender points, but Wickham's being anything but the black-hearted scoundrel he was? Well, that was at the very top.

"It is not that I do not care," Darcy muttered.

"Come along, Darcy. We did not ride over here to stand and gawk at the front door."

"I came with you because you wished it," Darcy grumbled as he followed Bingley into the house. "That is not what an unfeeling friend does."

"I will inform Mr. Bennet of that as soon as we are in his study unless, of course, you wish for me to announce it to the whole house."

"No, I do not wish for you to do that." He snapped as he handed his outerwear to a footman. "Insufferable," he muttered.

"You may tell Mr. Bennet that as well," Bingley assured him, earning for himself a well-deserved glare. "Mr. Hill, will you please inform the ladies that I will not leave without seeing them?"

"Of course, sir," Mr. Hill said.

Bingley glanced over his shoulder to ensure that Darcy was following him to Mr. Bennet's study and not gathering his things and leaving.

"Would you care for a glass of port or a cup of tea?" Mr. Bennet asked as Bingley and Darcy entered his office. He shuffled some papers around on his desk before taking a seat. "We also have coffee left from my breakfast because I always prefer a second cup after I return from my ride."

"Do you ride every morning?" Bingley asked. He had not thought of Mr. Bennet as one who liked to move very far from his study.

"Not every day," the man answered. "Sometimes I take a meander through the country, sometimes with my gun and sometimes with just my thoughts. Coffee?" he asked once again.

"Yes, thank you, coffee would be most welcome," Darcy replied. His tone still held a note of displeasure that Bingley found oddly delightful, even if he knew he likely should not feel so.

"And for you as well, Mr. Bingley?"

Bingley nodded. "Please. I have assured Darcy that I would tell you that it is not that he does not care about sharing in my joy. He did, after all, come with me today to give his congratulations to Miss Bennet and your wife."

Darcy turned wide eyes to Bingley. Darcy had not told him anything of the sort, but he knew Darcy. Darcy was not the sort to greet Miss Bennet or her mother without doing what was right and proper and that meant he would be extending his felicitations.

Mr. Bennet settled back into his chair and propped his elbows on the arms of the chair. "If he cares, then, why would he leave?"

The man was not reticent in his provocations, that was for certain. Bingley wondered for a moment if Mr. Bennet was the same with everyone or if just he knew that his friend needed the prodding.

"Do you wish to answer that, or should I?" Bingley asked Darcy.

Darcy expelled a breath. "Have you heard tales about me from Mr. Wickham?"

Mr. Bennet shook his head. "I heard Mr. Wickham's tales from Lizzy, but Mr. Wickham, himself, has not shared anything about you with me." His eyes shifted for a brief moment to Bingley before returning to Darcy. "I have, however, heard some details of your relationship with Mr. Wickham from your friend, and I understand you have good reason to not like the man. That being said, those reasons do not automatically refute all that Mr. Wickham has said. The best lies are the ones that contain bits and pieces of the truth."

"There is little truth in what Wickham says. I will own that I am not the most open and welcoming person at times, and I will not deny that I have extraordinarily little desire to attend a ball of any sort, even one hosted by my friend in celebration of his happy future." Darcy's eyes did not waver from their fixed gaze on Mr. Bennet. "Some, such as my friend here, would say I am reserved to a fault. I will give him that he is likely correct on that. Be that as it may, my refusal to stay in the area for longer than today has nothing to do with my dislike for society or from some imagined lack of compassion for Bingley's delight in securing Miss Bennet."

"I am to gather then, that your reason is Mr. Wickham?"

"Yes, it is," Darcy said. "It is not beneath him to do harm to my friends, simply because they are my friends. My removal from Netherfield is for the protection of those friends."

The rims of Darcy's ears were red. That was likely because he was treading precariously close to admitting that he considered Miss Elizabeth as a friend worthy of protection.

Mr. Bennet smiled. "And am I supposed to believe it is just for Mr. Bingley's protection that you are quitting the area?"

Darcy shook his head. "No, you are to make the necessary connections. Miss Bennet will eventually be Mrs. Bingley. She and all her sisters are now of importance to the scoundrel. Did Bingley mention anything to you about my sister?"

Mr. Bennet nodded. "In general terms."

"I have refused Wickham both a living, which he had previously rejected, and my sister's thirty thousand pounds."

Mr. Bennet's eyes widened at the sum.

"He has ample reason to wish to make me suffer for denying him such things," Darcy continued. "That is why I did not leave this morning as I had intended. Miss Bennet has told Bingley that Mr. Wickham has mentioned my sister in his stories. I need to know what he has said."

Understanding suffused Mr. Bennet's face and compassion touched his eyes. "Your sister's reputation is not damaged. He has only said that she is cold."

"Georgiana cold?" Darcy scoffed. "Hardly. Which is why he was able to play with her heart as he did."

"He likens her disposition to yours." Mr. Bennet gave Darcy a very pointed look. "And since my daughter's first encounter with you involved a stinging reproach, I am certain you can understand how she might be easily led to believe that your sister is not a warm and welcoming young lady but rather above all she meets, much like her brother."

Darcy's expression when he turned to Bingley could only be described as one of horror at what Mr. Bennet had said.

"She heard you," Bingley explained.

"And has shared it with several friends and relations," Mr. Bennet added. "So, she is not the only one convinced that you find her merely tolerable and not worthy of partnering for a dance."

"But it is not true," Darcy returned.

"Then, you find her handsome?" Mr. Bennet asked.

"Who would not?" Darcy answered.

"Lizzy's beauty pales when compared to Jane," Mr. Bennet replied.

Darcy shook his head. "I do not see how."

Mr. Bennet's lips twitched in restrained amusement. "Her mother has always proclaimed it, and it is Jane on whom the young men wish to call."

Darcy's head shook again as if he could not believe it.

"And then, there is the fact that I have indulged Lizzy's love of learning and turned her into a bit of a challenging young woman. Not that her natural temperament did not already lean in that direction. She was not an easy infant. Providing her with things to learn kept her entertained."

"And has made her a most interesting conversation partner. She debates quite well," Darcy said.

Mr. Bennet chuckled. "Debates or argues? She may have just been disagreeing with you because she was – is – angry with you for your comment." He shook his head. "Angry is probably what she thinks she is. Hurt is how I would say it."

Darcy glowered at Bingley. "I must apologize. I did not intend to injure your daughter," he said to Mr. Bennet.

"I can see that, and I am positive she has been told that very thing by Jane. However..."

Darcy nodded. "I know. I must apologize to her."

"I am afraid you must," Mr. Bennet agreed. "And by doing so, perhaps you can displace Mr. Wickham in her esteem. She is smart enough to see through his lies, but I fear she is not thinking clearly." He blew out a great breath. "And we could use any assistance in discrediting Mr. Wickham that you could afford us."

Bingley sat forward. "Why?"

"I have let it be known that he is fond of flirting – or more – with any willing young ladies, and I have shared that he is known for creating debts he cannot pay." He grimaced. "However, it seems that Mr. Wickham fell into some luck during a card game recently and there are very few bills he has not paid."

"What?" Bingley cried. "He did not ignore his bills in pursuit of pleasure?"

Mr. Bennet shook his head. "Miss King is to inherit a tidy sum upon her grandfather's death, and the old gentleman is not the sort who would allow anyone to call on his granddaughter if the man did not present himself as financially responsible and dedicated to circumspect behaviour toward young ladies."

"But surely, Wickham has been seen with some maid."

Mr. Bennet shrugged. "Sir William had not heard of any, and from the way things appear, neither has Mr. King."

Bingley fell back in his chair. What were they to do now? How could they get rid of Wickham and prove to Miss Elizabeth that he was a scoundrel if the man insisted on changing tack and playing the part of an honorable gent?

Chapter 5

A HALF AN HOUR later, Bingley and Darcy had finished their coffee and their discussion with Mr. Bennet. The man was quite knowledgeable on several topics. Bingley had done more listening to his friend and Mr. Bennet discuss books and the struggles that come with estate stewardship than he had talking. That had been an excellent thing since his mind had been occupied with trying to figure out a way to get rid of Wickham or to keep Darcy in the area if ridding it of Wickham was not a possibility.

"I wish you well in your quest, Mr. Darcy," Mr. Bennet said when Bingley stood and Darcy followed suit. "Elizabeth's opinion is not always easily swayed." He leaned to the side as he looked up from his place behind his desk at Bingley and Darcy. "You may have to prove to her that you are the opposite of what Mr. Wickham said."

Darcy nodded slowly. "I know."

"Especially since her opinion of your sister is based on her opinion of you."

"I am aware of that, as well."

"You know..." Mr. Bennet suddenly found several papers on his desk that needed attention. "There is something you could do which might guarantee, at least, a small reversal of her displeasure."

Darcy's head cocked to one side. "What is that?"

Mr. Bennet peeked up at Darcy with a cunning smile. "Attend a ball."

"I –" Darcy began to refute but Mr. Bennet kept speaking.

"Bring your sister so that Elizabeth can see for herself that Miss Darcy is not what Mr. Wickham says. And make sure you secure the first and supper dances with Elizabeth."

Oh, the man was brilliant! How had he come to that conclusion while he was carrying on a discussion with Darcy? Bingley smiled broadly. Approaching Mr. Bennet for assistance had been a capital idea. He would have to congratulate himself properly for his decision with a glass of port later.

"Two sets?" Darcy looked from the man behind the desk to Bingley and back. "That would be raising expectations."

Mr. Bennet shrugged. "My expectations are already high since you have just today admitted that you find my daughter beautiful and that you admire her mind."

Darcy shook his head. "I cannot attend Bingley's ball."

"I am afraid it might be the only way to clear your name."

"Indeed," Bingley agreed eagerly. This was a fabulous plan! "You did say Miss Elizabeth was not pretty enough to tempt you into dancing."

"I danced with her at your last ball," Darcy growled.

"Yes, you did, which raises my expectations higher," Mr. Bennet said.

Darcy dropped back down into the chair from which he had only moments before risen. "I cannot bring Georgiana to Netherfield. Wickham is still in the area."

Mr. Bennet leaned forward and shook his head. "That matters not. Consider what we know about his recent behaviour."

Bingley gasped as full understanding dawned on him. Mr. Bennet's scheme kept getting better and better. "Wickham would not want to do anything to offend Mr. King."

"Precisely."

"We cannot play to his deceit," Darcy said emphatically. "Mr. King should be made aware of Wickham's nature, although I do not know how to do it without putting my sister at risk."

"He has a point," Bingley said. Darcy often had good points, and, on occasions, such as this one, they thwarted Bingley's plans. It was because Darcy rarely became so narrowly focused on the end result as Bingley did, for Darcy was the sort of fellow who paused to determine the pitfalls and disasters before he began.

"That is just it," Mr. Bennet said. "By playing to Mr. Wickham's deception and, in the process, proving yourself to be the opposite of what he said you were, you will expose him, and your sister will remain safe."

"That is also a good point." And a point that Bingley liked a lot better than Darcy's because it would help bring the result Bingley sought.

Mr. Bennet held up his hands when Darcy began to shake his head.

"Just think about it," Mr. Bennet said. "That is all I ask."

"Wise advice." Once again, and before Darcy could toss out any other challenges, Bingley rose to bring an end to the conversation. "While you are thinking, I suggest we seek out Miss Bennet and her sister so that you can apologize."

Darcy's head swung back and forth. "Not so I can apologize. So that we can apologize. I am not claiming your portion of the responsibility for this misunderstanding."

Mr. Bennet chuckled. "That is a most excellent point, Mr. Darcy. Would you not agree, Mr. Bingley?"

"Without a doubt." He had planned to stand with Darcy during his apology. First, to provide assurance to Miss Elizabeth that what Darcy said was true, and then, to make sure Darcy did not say or do anything that would further hinder the chances of Miss Elizabeth coming to admit her admiration of the man.

"There is always a chair in here for either of you gentlemen, and Mr. Darcy," Mr. Bennet called as Bingley and Darcy were just about to exit.

"Yes?"

"I would not refuse you if you find you wish to ask my daughter for something longer lasting than a dance. You would make a fine son."

"He feels the honour of your trust," Bingley replied with a wink for Mr. Bennet as he pulled his startled friend from the room.

"A fine son," Darcy muttered once the door to the study had been closed and the two of them had begun moving down the corridor. "I am not even asking for a dance, so there is little chance I will be asking her to marry me." He shook his head. "I should have stayed in London."

"Come along, old man. You have a lady to unoffend."

Darcy turned in front of Bingley and stopped him with a firm hand to the chest. They were now just past the stairway and nearly to the sitting room door.

"May we now stop that foolish game you enjoy so much?" Darcy demanded.

"You do not protest it all that much."

"I protest it every time you propose it."

"And yet you participate."

"Under duress."

"I never threaten you." Bingley folded his arms. "What hardship will you face if you refuse to play?"

"I will have to tell you the truth outright instead of concealing it, for you will not stop badgering me to do what I do not wish to do just because I said I do not wish to play your game. You knew why I was in no humor to dance, and yet you persisted."

Darcy's voice had risen to a loud whisper. He was thoroughly agitated, and Bingley should likely have ended his prodding there. However, two pretty ladies had appeared on the stairway behind Darcy, and a perfect way to begin changing Miss Elizabeth's mind about Darcy appeared with them.

"Let me see if I understand you. Are you telling me that you would have preferred to say that Miss Elizabeth was alluringly beautiful and that your attraction to her made you fear dancing with her? Is that what you are saying?"

"Yes, that is it precisely, for if I had, she would not have been injured by my words which would have been injurious to anyone, who did not know we were playing a game." He shook his head. "I have truly never been so ashamed of myself. To have made Miss Elizabeth think that she is anything other than perhaps the most beautiful lady in

England." Again, his head shook from side to side. "And to have lied – even if part of a game. It is reprehensible."

Miss Elizabeth stood frozen, with her mouth agape, on the stairs next to Miss Bennet, who was covering a broad smile with her hand.

"Well, then, I suppose, since you now know that she heard you at the assembly, we should get on with finding Miss Elizabeth so you can apologize for your disparagement, and," his eyes held Miss Elizabeth's, "so I can apologize for the game you played to humor me. There never was a better friend, Darcy. I know how much you despise deception and disguise."

"Does this mean you will not harass me to do things I do not wish to do?"

Bingley chuckled and shook his head. "That I cannot promise, for it is often how I get you to do the uncomfortable. And you are sometimes grateful afterward."

"Only sometimes." Darcy's expression was hard.

"You know I will not be able to stop completely, do you not?"

Darcy closed his eyes and expelled a great sigh. "Yes. I am just thankful that your portion of the Bingley charm has never devolved into scheming to see me married or to speaking ill of others like your sisters do."

If the man only knew. Of course, he would in a moment.

"I, myself, am grateful that I am not so mean and small-minded as Caroline and Louisa can be. However, I reserve the right to scheme a bit if it ensures your happiness."

One of Darcy's eyebrows arched. "Elaborate."

"I would only attempt to arrange things for you if I knew your heart about a lady."

Darcy's eyes grew wide. "Is that why I am here? Is this all an extravagant ruse?"

"Why would I conspire to bring you here?"

Darcy leaned forward and spoke in a low rumble, "You know how I feel about Miss Elizabeth, for you extracted that information from me two nights ago. Had you been less angry, you might not know it now, but you do."

Bingley glanced at the ladies on the stairs. Poor Miss Elizabeth looked ready to faint away. He sent a pleading look to Jane to come to his assistance.

"Mr. Bingley, Mr. Darcy," she said sweetly as she descended the final portion of the stairs. Her steps were light and without sound, "Mr. Hill said you would stop to see us before you left. I am happy to see he was correct."

Darcy grasped Bingley's arm. There was a panicked question in his eyes to which Bingley nodded in reply.

"I would only ever scheme if it gave you a chance at happiness," he whispered. "Mr. Darcy might wish for a chair and a glass of wine," he said brightly to Jane.

"I think some air might be better," Darcy muttered.

"You told Mr. Bennet you wished to extend your congratulations to Miss Bennet and her mother."

"No, you told him that," Darcy hissed through clenched teeth.

"There will be no fisticuff in the hallway," Jane said as she came to stand next to Darcy. "I will tell my mother that Mr. Bingley wished to walk in the garden and that I asked Elizabeth to accompany us. I will also make sure she knows you are happy to hear that her daughter is marrying your friend. Would that be acceptable to you, Mr. Darcy?"

"Yes."

"My sister and I will meet you in the garden."

Darcy nodded and turned around slowly. "Miss Elizabeth," he greeted with a tip of his head.

"No fisticuffs," Jane reminded him. "Mr. Hill, the gentlemen require their things," she added before she stepped into the drawing room.

"Will you join me in the garden?" Darcy asked Miss Elizabeth. "It seems there are things about which we need to speak."

"You like me?" Her eyes registered her confusion.

Darcy swallowed and nodded. "Please, may we speak in the garden, and, if you wish to send me away, you can do it there?"

"Of course," she replied. "I will get my coat and bonnet." She turned from him and took two steps up the stairs before looking back at him. "It was a game?"

"Not a very good game," Bingley interjected. "But yes. I do hope you can find it in your heart to forgive us."

She nodded, and then, tipping her head studied Darcy for a moment before continuing up the stairs.

"You knew she was behind me?" There was a bit of venom in Darcy's whisper.

Fisticuff might not happen in the garden, but Bingley was not certain he was going to survive this bit of trickery without some damage to his person.

"You needed to apologize, and I thought it the best way for Miss Elizabeth to believe every word you said if you said it without knowing she could hear it."

Darcy made a displeased sound. "Why do I keep you as a friend?"

"I have no idea," Bingley admitted. "But I am most heartily grateful that you do. You will still l keep me as a friend, will you not?" he added as he hurried out of the house behind Darcy.

Darcy turned toward Bingley. "For the life of me, I do not know why, but yes, you may remain my friend." He scrubbed his face. "However, that may become a very difficult thing should Miss Elizabeth send me away."

Chapter 6

BINGLEY RUBBED HIS HANDS together and paced a few steps away from where Darcy was doing the same thing. It was not the warmest day. Hopefully, Jane and her sister would not become too chilled.

"My mother wishes to thank Mr. Darcy for his kind regard," Jane said as she reached where Bingley and Darcy were pacing. "She hopes you will both be able to join her for a cup of tea after our walk. However, I told her I did not know your plans and could only promise to extend the invitation."

Ah, he was marrying a wise lady! If things did not go well, Darcy would not wish to sit in the sitting room and listen to Mrs. Bennet, and Bingley would wish to follow Darcy back to Netherfield.

"Darcy plans to return to London on the morrow, so we may not be able to accept her hospitality as our time is limited to see to what needs seeing to. Indeed, I do not even know what that entails precisely, so our schedule is at Darcy's discretion." Bingley offered his arm to Jane.

"This path is closely watched," he said to Darcy. "It might be best if you and Miss Elizabeth walked separately as not to draw too much notice."

Miss Elizabeth was standing at Darcy's side but with her hands clasped behind her back as if she was very uneasy to be where she was. Could Bingley be so fortunate that such unease was due more to a stirring of affection towards his friend rather than mere embarrassment? There was no way to be certain, but Bingley decided it would be best to decide on the side of affection since that was the desired outcome.

"Is that what you would prefer, Miss Elizabeth?" Darcy asked.

She nodded. "It seems best. I have no desire to answer questions from my mother if I can avoid it."

Darcy smiled at her and his eyes took in her features before he turned away. He was utterly smitten with Miss Elizabeth, which meant it was imperative that this discussion go well. Bingley would hate to be the source of heartbreak for his friend. He likely should have thought about that sooner, but he had not. Therefore, if this was to be a tale cast at his feet, he might as well take charge of the whole of it and earn either the accolades or lamentations.

"Miss Elizabeth," Bingley began, "I must apologize for all the animosity between yourself and my friend since our arrival in Hertfordshire. I assure you that Darcy does not, as a practice, speak ill of ladies or gentlemen within their hearing."

Her eyebrows rose over an accusatory expression.

"We all have our moments in private, of course, when we comment on someone's attire or the dreadfully dull conversation we endured. Darcy is no different, but he does not offend just to be offensive."

"Bingley," Darcy inserted in a pleading tone.

"He does have a tendency to offend by accident, but I assure you it is only on occasion."

"Why do I keep you as a friend?" Darcy rumbled.

Miss Elizabeth's lips twitched in amusement as Bingley continued to ignore his friend.

"Surely, if Darcy were the sort to offend without conscience, would he not have made sport of your cousin, Mr. Collins, at my last ball? I mean no offense, but I do think if any gentleman has ever lain himself open for ridicule, it is Mr. Collins."

"Allow me," Jane said softly before Bingley could elaborate on his meaning further.

He nodded his acceptance.

"I believe what Mr. Bingley is attempting to say is that Mr. Darcy is an honorable gentleman who does not deal lightly with the sensibilities of others. He measures his words on most occasions but, as happens with all of us, is not without fault."

"Yes, yes," Bingley agreed heartily. "That is it precisely. And when he does err, he feels it most grievously." He once again congratulated himself on choosing such a wise lady to be his wife.

"Which," Jane continued, "is what I have been telling you for months now."

Elizabeth smiled sheepishly at the pointed comment. "Yes, you have said that, but you have also had Mr. Bingley's ear."

"Have I ever tried to maneuver things to my advantage?" There was a sharp edge to Jane's question.

"No," Elizabeth replied with what appeared to be reluctance.

"I am grieved to have caused you pain," Darcy said. "It was badly done. Badly done, indeed."

"The game is of my creation," Bingley said. "Darcy humors me."

"Yes, I heard that when you were talking in the hall," Elizabeth said.

They had reached the secluded corner of the garden with its trees and bushes that stood sentry against the breeze, making this corner much more pleasant than the rest of the garden on a day such as today.

"What I struggle with at present is Mr. Darcy's opinion of me, for it is far from what I had thought it to be," she continued. "I assumed he watched me to find fault."

"I watched with admiration," Darcy's voice was quiet. It had to be difficult to admit such personal things with an audience, even if that audience was only two people.

Elizabeth held Darcy's gaze, and Bingley held his breath as he waited to hear her reply. Much to his surprise, she did not pursue the topic further. Once again, he hoped it was due to her admiration of Darcy.

"Why did you leave Netherfield? Was it to separate my sister from your friend?" Her look was challenging.

Darcy nodded. "It was. However, it is not for the reasons you might suppose."

"It truly is not," Jane added her assurance. "Mr. Bingley has told me why you left," she explained to Darcy. "You have nothing to fear from me. I have not and will not reveal your secret to anyone."

"Secret? What secret?" Miss Elizabeth looked from her sister to Darcy.

"I am sure it comes as no surprise to you that Darcy and Mr. Wickham are not on friendly terms," Bingley said.

"That is putting it gently," Darcy agreed. He turned to Miss Elizabeth again. "I do not know in detail what Mr. Wickham has told you about me, but I will assure you that only portions of it are true. He was the son of my father's steward. He was also my father's godson and favoured. Indeed, he was favoured enough to be provided for in my father's will."

"Quite well provided for," Bingley inserted. "However, he refused to take orders for he thought the law suited him better."

"And in place of the living," Darcy said, "I gave him a sum of money to see him settled into his new life. He wasted it on living in a way that is not fitting for me to share with you, and when the money was gone, he came to me, asking to be given the living he had once refused. I did not give it to him. He was not fit for the church."

"And he had already been given money in place of it," Bingley inserted just for emphasis of that important point.

"Mr. Wickham refused the living at first?" Miss Elizabeth asked.

"Yes," Darcy replied.

"And he was not left without any inheritance?"

"No."

"Therefore, you did not dishonour your father's wishes?"

Darcy shook his head. "I never would." He drew a breath. "As you can imagine, Mr. Wickham was not pleased to be refused the living and abused me grievously regarding it. However, his stories and cutting remarks were nothing compared to how he tried to exact his revenge."

Miss Elizabeth's eyes were wide.

"I have a sister, as I know Mr. Wickham has told you."

Miss Elizabeth's hand rested on her heart as she nodded. Bingley could see the trepidation in her eyes as she waited to hear the horrid tale Darcy was about to reveal.

"She is just recently turned sixteen and is the sweetest of young ladies with a heart that is of the tenderest kind. Wickham gained access to her through a companion that my cousin and I had hired for Georgiana. He followed them to Ramsgate last summer and ingratiated himself to my sister with stories of our father and his times at Pemberley. I had never told my sister about Wickham's true nature. I did not think it was appropriate for her to hear, and I saw no need for the disclosure. I was wrong in that. She had no warning of what he was like, and he was persuasive enough that she supposed herself in love with him."

Miss Elizabeth expelled a breath as if she had been knocked in the abdomen.

"It was only by the grace of Providence that I travelled to Ramsgate earlier than expected and discovered their plan to elope." Darcy shook his head and turned slightly away.

Bingley picked up the story for his friend. "Wickham's goals were Miss Darcy's thirty thousand pounds and to deal a devastating blow to his childhood friend, whom he now considered his adversary."

"If he had succeeded," Darcy whispered.

"But he did not," Bingley inserted. "Miss Darcy is safe, though recovering from a broken heart, and Darcy is fearful of anyone, for whom he cares, being treated just as shabbily by Wickham as Miss Darcy was. That is why he left Netherfield and attempted to separate me from Jane. He feared for me, your sister, and you, as well as your family. He still fears Wickham might try to harm your family because, in harming a family tied to me, Darcy's dearest friend, he would strike a blow at Darcy himself."

Miss Elizabeth shook her head. "Is this all true?"

"Sadly, yes," Darcy answered.

"One of my purposes in returning to Hertfordshire was to try to discredit Wickham," Bingley said. Now was the time to lay the details of his plan before them all and let the results be what they would be. "I told your father in general terms about Wickham's history with Darcy. He planned to spread some gossip about Wickham's penchant to seduce young ladies and leave bills unpaid, and we hoped that it would drive him from the area."

"I do not understand. Why would you wish to drive him from the area? Would it not be enough for my father to know that Mr. Wickham is not to be trusted?"

Bingley shook his head. "I needed him to leave the area for the rest of my plan to work."

Darcy's left eyebrow cocked in interest.

"Darcy wanted to introduce his sister to you."

"To me?" Miss Elizabeth repeated in disbelief as Darcy closed his eyes and grimaced.

"Yes. Because he was so enamoured with you that he was thinking beyond friendship or even courtship."

"Bingley." Darcy begged him with that one word to stop, but Bingley was not about to do so.

Miss Elizabeth's lips were slightly parted, and her brow was deeply creased in disbelief.

"I assure you it is true, and I am likely taking my wellbeing into my own hands to share all this. When I discovered Darcy's thoughts and wishes regarding you and how he was denying them to see that you were kept safe..."

Ah, there was an encouraging sight. Miss Elizabeth had turned to look at Darcy in wonder.

"I decided to do what I could to see him happy. Therefore, I returned to Netherfield with the intent of securing Jane and planning a ball, which I hoped would bring Darcy back and that he would bring his sister with him."

"And then you, my dear sister," Jane inserted, "would see that Mr. Wickham had lied to you about Miss Darcy, and seeing that truth, coupled with Mr. Darcy's eagerness to make his sister known to you, you would be swayed from your stubborn dislike of him." She left Bingley's side and went to her sister. "Do you still insist upon disliking him?" She took Elizabeth's hand. "He has never thought of you as merely tolerable. Can you let go of your injured pride and hurt to learn about who Mr. Darcy really is? I am marrying his dearest friend after all."

Elizabeth nodded slowly. "How can I cling to something as truth when it has been proven false?"

Bingley sighed in relief. He had succeeded – at least, in part.

"I think it is only right that I give Mr. Darcy the opportunity to show me who he truly is," Elizabeth added.

"You will give me a second chance?"

Bingley nearly chuckled at the eagerness in his friend's voice.

"I will."

"You will?"

"Yes, Mr. Darcy, I will. However, we are off to a very shaky beginning if you are going to insist upon questioning everything I say." Her eyes twinkled with amusement, but she tucked the corner of her lip between her teeth nervously.

"I apologize. I did not mean to question you so much as to question my good fortune." He glanced at Bingley. "May I secure two dances from you for Bingley's ball?"

"You are planning to attend?" Bingley could not believe what he was hearing. He had been certain he would need to work on Darcy a bit more before the man would be persuaded to attend his ball.

"I am, so long as I can dance the first and supper sets with Miss Elizabeth." He took a step closer to Elizabeth. "May I have those dances?"

Elizabeth's eyes did not waver from their fixed gaze on Darcy's as she nodded her acceptance.

"And I can introduce you to my sister?"

Again, the question was met with a nod of approval.

It was all done. That which Bingley had set out to do was complete – well, Darcy was not yet betrothed, but it most certainly seemed as if he had a good chance of becoming so shortly. Therefore, Bingley was going to count his task as successfully completed and reward himself by enjoying a cup of tea and the warmth of a fire with Jane. "Shall we go in search of a cup of tea now?" he asked.

"I would like that," Darcy said as he extended his arm to Miss Elizabeth, who to Bingley's utter delight, accepted it without hesitation.

Chapter 7

BINGLEY STOOD AT NETHERFIELD'S drawing room window, looking toward the drive. Behind him, Darcy sat discussing Elizabeth with his sister, Georgiana, and their cousin, Colonel Richard Fitzwilliam, who had joined Darcy as an extra layer of protection against Wickham doing something stupid.

Over the course of the two and a half weeks that Darcy had stayed at Netherfield before departing to collect his sister, Bingley had insisted that they call on as many of the neighbours as was possible so that one and all could see that Darcy was not the cold and uncaring person Wickham had touted him to be. He had also insisted that Darcy be seen in Meryton twice with Elizabeth – once in a carriage and once while walking the streets and visiting the shops. And then, there had been church, where each Sunday, Darcy had sat with Bingley, but immediately upon completion of the service, sought out Miss Elizabeth. Bingley wished he could take credit for that action as it had set several tongues to wagging immediately, but he could not. That was entirely Darcy's doing.

Elizabeth also played her part well, though she neither knew she was playing a part nor how she was to play it.

She just naturally grew to favour Darcy and to smile at him whenever he was near. She had even smiled across the church at him. That had not gone unnoticed by the matrons who kept everyone abreast of the important happenings in the neighborhood. Bingley had heard it whispered from one lady to another – both speculating on the possibility of a second Bennet wedding – before Darcy had reached Elizabeth's side that first Sunday.

Darcy had only returned yesterday, but he had not spent a minute longer than necessary to deposit his relations at Netherfield before he was off to Longbourn to inform Mrs. Bennet that he was safely returned and to invite Elizabeth to meet his sister before the ball.

Bingley had heard whispers from his servants that Mr. Darcy had returned with a beautiful ring in his possession. Things were just as they should be, for Bingley also knew, from Jane, that Elizabeth would not refuse an offer from Darcy. Of course, he shared that information with no one. It was his and Jane's secret.

He shifted to make himself somewhat more comfortable as he stared out into the dim shadows of the evening, searching for the first sign that Jane and her sister had arrived. The carriage would return to Longbourn to collect the rest of the Bennet family. It was just Jane and Elizabeth who were expected at present. A light meal awaited them. It was not much. It was only to be sustenance to tide everyone over until supper later in the night.

Seeing no carriage, Bingley's mind shifted back to his success in completing what he had set out from London to do when he returned to Netherfield three weeks ago.

Mr. King had been on the list of neighbours for him and Darcy to visit. The elderly gentleman had been quite impressed with Darcy. Bingley knew he was because he had mentioned it twice to his granddaughter by way of a "This, Mary, is the way a young man should be. You'd do much better to set your cap at a fine gentleman such as Mr. Darcy instead of some officer with charming looks and pretty words."

Mr. King and his granddaughter would be at Bingley's ball, but Wickham would not be. Mr. King had raised a quizzical brow when he had heard that Wickham's omission from the guest list was due to some unfavorable dealing between Wickham and Darcy, as well as his cousin, the Earl of Matlock's second son, who would also be in attendance at the ball.

It would not be long before Wickham would find himself seeking another lady to charm, for Bingley was certain that Mr. King was not the sort of gentleman to allow his granddaughter to keep company with a fellow who was kept from society due to having caused some sort of offense to a member of an earl's family.

A carriage turned into the drive.

Bingley clapped his hands and turned from the window. "They are here."

Georgiana joined him at the window to peek out at the carriage and catch a glimpse of Jane and Elizabeth. She looked a trifle uneasy, but her brother seemed perfectly at case – much as he did when he was at his own home. It was not how Darcy normally appeared before a social function. Miss Elizabeth had wrought a remarkable transformation in the man.

Richard joined Georgiana at the window. "The one in the blue pelisse?" he looked at Bingley. "Is that the lady I will be calling cousin?"

Georgiana gasped and turned to her brother. "Are you going to marry her?"

"Why else would he have you meet her?" Richard answered.

"I have not asked her," Darcy said from where he sat, "but that is the hope."

"I do hope, even more now than I did a minute ago, that I like her," Georgiana said with one last look out the window before returning to her seat.

"You will," Darcy assured her. "You have not found anything to fault in all that I have told you about her."

"And Darcy is not given to liking dreadful chits," Richard added, earning himself a giggle from Georgiana.

"Do you suppose she will like me?" Georgiana asked.

"How could she not?" Richard said as they all stood to welcome the Miss Bennets.

It was as Georgiana hoped. She was welcomed readily by Elizabeth and found herself enamoured with the lady who would be her sister.

"Do you think you will be allowed to attend the ball?" Jane asked when Darcy had excused himself and Elizabeth to speak privately.

Georgiana pulled her eyes away from watching the door to the drawing room for the return of her brother. Excitement seemed to bubble within her for Bingley had never seen her expression so animated.

"I am allowed to attend, but I am not to dance with anyone other than my cousin, my brother, and Mr. Bingley."

"I am happy to hear you will not be shut up in your room while we are having a grand time in the ballroom. That would be most miserable."

"Indeed, it would be," Richard agreed. "I had almost expected Darcy to forbid her attendance, but he is changed."

"Indeed, he is," Georgiana agreed. "He seems happy."

"And at peace," Richard added. "It seems your betrothed has worked a bit of good for him."

Jane looked at Bingley with a sweet smile and took his hand. "I am fortunate to be marrying such a clever man, am I not?"

"How was he clever?" Georgiana asked.

This led to a relation of all that had happened in the past three weeks.

"Did Fitzwilliam harm you for causing him such embarrassment? He is not usually given to violence, but I have seen him come to blows with his cousins."

"No, Miss Darcy," Bingley replied, "I was saved from any unsavoury consequences by Miss Elizabeth's willingness to give your brother a second chance."

"Do you think she will accept his offer of marriage?" Georgiana asked in a whisper.

"I dare say she will unless your brother makes a muck of it." Bingley rose and pulled Jane to her feet. "Come with me, my darling Jane. We must eat soon and there is not too overly long before all must be in place for the ball. I think it is best if we make certain Darcy does not destroy the festive atmosphere before it has even begun."

Richard chuckled.

"You do not mind if we leave you for a few minutes?" Bingley asked.

"No, but do hurry back with any good news," Georgiana answered.

"It is the only sort of news I will accept," Bingley assured her.

He was mostly confident that Darcy could propose to Elizabeth without issue, but there was a small niggling uneasiness that remained. One must not allow one's plan to unravel if one could do something to ensure it did not.

"Stewart," Bingley called to the footman who was carrying a basket of greenery and oranges to the front entrance.

"Yes, sir."

Stewart had yet to look at his employer without a wary look, and Bingley had yet to teach him billiards.

"Do you know where Mr. Darcy is?"

There was the smallest tipping up of Stewart's lips on the right side.

"He is in the library, but I am not certain he wishes for company."

Ah! That was promising. Very promising, indeed.

"The door is open?"

"Yes, sir."

"Good. Then, we will not disturb him unless he appears to need the distraction." He allowed Stewart to continue on his way before pulling Jane closer to his side and whispering, "It sounds as if I am worried for no reason."

"It does sound that way," she agreed. "And I do hope it is true."

"You are not opposed to peeking in on them, are you?"

"Not at all. I am particularly good at stealing a look to see what my sisters are about."

He chuckled. "So am I."

"Have you heard from your sisters again?"

"Yes, just yesterday. That makes four very unhappy letters. They are still displeased that I am not going to join them for Christmas and that I refuse to invite them to Netherfield. I have already told them that they are not welcome until the wedding breakfast and then, they must return to town that same day. I will not relent too soon when it comes to making them feel the consequences of their actions towards you."

He was certain he would get an even more scathing letter in reply to the one he intended to send tomorrow informing them of the success of his ball – the one they still knew nothing about – and of Mr. Darcy's betrothal to Miss Elizabeth. Once again, he almost wished he could be there to witness the looks on their faces when they discovered he had hosted a soiree on his own and that Mr. Darcy was no longer a free man.

He chuckled to himself.

"What is so humorous?"

"I was just thinking about how disappointed Caroline will be when I write to her about that." He nodded to the library, where Darcy and Elizabeth were wrapped in each other's embrace and obviously not desirous of any company, save their own.

"Oh! I am so happy."

"As am I, my darling Jane." Bingley pulled a small branch of mistletoe from his pocket and drew Jane to himself. "My excuse should someone see us," he said as he lifted the sprig of mistletoe above Jane's head.

To his surprise, she leaned forward and placed a kiss on his lips. He returned the action when she pulled back. And as he revelled in his good fortune, the mistletoe found itself discarded on the floor so that he could use both arms to hold his beloved.

Tonight, he would dance with the lady who loved him and whom he loved in return.

Mr. Bennet would make a toast to not only he and Jane but also to Darcy and Elizabeth, while Mrs. Bennet would be nearly overcome with the delight of it all and need her salts and an extra glass of wine.

Georgiana would safely and happily dance at her first ball, once with each of her approved partners, and then, she would make the acquaintance of a pleasant young fellow who was only in the area to visit his aunt for Christmas but who would be happy to save a dance for her next season. (And he would be true to his word.)

Miss King would find a delightful reason to forget Wickham when the colonel found himself enamoured with a lady who dressed a bit out of date and discussed things as if she had years of wisdom upon which to draw, though she was only twenty-five. They would spend two sets dancing and several more talking as they watched others dance. They would not, however, marry because life would, once Christmas was over, take them in very different directions. Yet, the tide for Wickham where Miss King was concerned had turned, for why would a lady such as herself settle for a lieutenant when she could inspire such attention from a colonel?

Eventually, as the snows of winter subsided, and the warmth of the sun returned, bringing with it the first blooms of spring, Bingley and Jane would stand in front of the parson alongside Darcy and Elizabeth, pledging their troths and binding themselves to one another forever.

And while his sisters would attend the wedding breakfast and pretend to be happy, Bingley would once again stand in the ballroom at Netherfield and congratulate himself for the good fortune he had found and for being the means of bringing the same to his friend.

Mr. Bennet would once again lift his glass to proclaim his delight about his daughters' futures in a toast that would end with how happy he was that, once upon a December day, Mr. Bingley had decided to plan a ball.

If you enjoyed this book, be sure to let others know by leaving a review.

Want to know when other Leenie books will be available?
You can always know what's new with my books by joining one of my reader communities

leeniebrown.com/subscribe

More Books by Leenie

You can find all of Leenie's books at this link

bit.ly/LeenieBBooks
where you can explore the collections below
~*~

Dash of Darcy and Companions Collection

Marrying Elizabeth Series

Sweet Possibilities and Sweet Extras

Willow Hall Romances

The Choices Series

Darcy Family Holidays

Darcy and... An Austen-Inspired Collection

Teatime Tales (Sweet Austen-inspired Novelettes)

Other Pens

Touches of Austen

Nature's Fury and Delights (Sweet Regency Novelettes)

About Leenie

Leenie Brown has always been a girl with an active imagination, which, while growing up, was both an asset, providing many hours of fun as she played out stories, and a liability, when her older sister and aunt would tell her frightening tales. At one time, they had her convinced Dracula lived in the trunk at the end of the bed she slept in when visiting her grandparents!

Although it has been years since she cowered in her bed in her grandparents' basement, she still has an imagination which occasionally runs away with her, and she feeds it now as she did then — by reading!

Her heroes, when growing up, were authors, and the worlds they painted with words were (and still are) her favourite playgrounds! Now, as an adult, she spends much of her time in the Regency world, playing with the characters from her favourite Jane Austen novels and those of her own creation.

When she is not traipsing down a trail in an attempt to keep up with her imagination, Leenie resides in the beautiful province of Nova Scotia with her two sons and her very own Mr. Brown (a wonderful mix of all the best of Darcy, Bingley, and Edmund with a healthy dose of the teasing Mr. Tilney and just a dash of the scolding Mr. Knightley).

Connect with Leenie in one of her reader communities or on social media. Find links to all of those on her website at bit.ly/connect-with-leenie